Dear Parents:

Congratulations! Your child is taking the first steps on an exciting journey. The destination? Independent reading!

STEP INTO READING® will help your child get there. The program offers five steps to reading success. Each step includes fun stories and colorful art or photographs. In addition to original fiction and books with favorite characters, there are Step into Reading Non-Fiction Readers, Phonics Readers and Boxed Sets, Sticker Readers, and Comic Readers—a complete literacy program with something to interest every child.

Learning to Read, Step by Step!

Ready to Read   Preschool–Kindergarten
• big type and easy words • rhyme and rhythm • picture clues
For children who know the alphabet and are eager to begin reading.

Reading with Help   Preschool–Grade 1
• basic vocabulary • short sentences • simple stories
For children who recognize familiar words and sound out new words with help.

Reading on Your Own   Grades 1–3
• engaging characters • easy-to-follow plots • popular topics
For children who are ready to read on their own.

Reading Paragraphs   Grades 2–3
• challenging vocabulary • short paragraphs • exciting stories
For newly independent readers who read simple sentences with confidence.

Ready for Chapters   Grades 2–4
• chapters • longer paragraphs • full-color art
For children who want to take the plunge into chapter books but still like colorful pictures.

STEP INTO READING® is designed to give every child a successful reading experience. The grade levels are only guides; children will progress through the steps at their own speed, developing confidence in their reading.

Remember, a lifetime love of reading starts with a single step!

All rights reserved. Published in the United States by Random House Children's Books,
a division of Penguin Random House LLC, New York. Featuring characters from *The Lorax,*
® & copyright © 1971, and copyright renewed 1999 by Dr. Seuss Enterprises, L.P.

Step into Reading, Random House, and the Random House colophon are registered trademarks
of Penguin Random House LLC.

Visit us on the Web!
Seussville.com
StepIntoReading.com
rhcbooks.com

Educators and librarians, for a variety of teaching tools, visit us at RHTeachersLibrarians.com

Library of Congress Cataloging-in-Publication Data is available upon request.
ISBN 978-0-593-56314-4 (trade) — ISBN 978-0-593-56315-1 (lib. bdg.)

Printed in the United States of America
10 9 8 7 6 5 4 3 2 1

COOKING
with the
LORAX

by Sonali Fry

illustrated by Anthony Conley

Random House 🏠 New York

I am the Lorax.
I want something
to munch.

I think that a salad
would make a good lunch.

Come with me.
I will share.
My garden is right
over there.

A salad needs some greens.

I pick lettuce and beans.

Carrots will add crunch.

I will pick a bunch!

Maybe a potato?

No . . . I do not think so.

I will gather berries.

I will pick some cherries.

I am done with my stroll.

Time to get the salad bowl.

Wash, wash, wash.

Slice, slice, slice.

Everything looks very nice!

Add a cheesy crumble.

Can you hear my
tummy rumble?

Pepper and salt,
if you please.

But not too much,
or I will sneeze!

Then a dressing goes
on top.

First, I like to taste
a drop.

Now I toss it
up, up high.
Watch the salad
fly, fly, fly!

28

Finally, my salad is done.
Making it was lots of fun!

A salad is a yummy

treat. . . .

I cannot wait to sit
and eat!